# GERALD McBOING BOING BOING

based on the Academy Award–winning motion picture by

## Dr. Seuss

pictures adapted by MEL CRAWFORD

RANDOM HOUSE 🏠 NEW YORK

This is the story of Gerald McCloy
And the strange thing that happened
to that little boy.

They say it all started
    when Gerald was two—
That's the age kids start talking—
    least, most of them do.
Well, when he started talking,
    you know what he said?

He didn't talk words—
he went BOING BOING! instead!
"What's that?" cried his father,
his face turning gray,
"That's a very odd thing
for a young boy to say!"

And poor Gerald's father
  rushed to the phone
And quick dialed the number
  of Doctor Malone.
"Come over fast!"
  the poor father pled.
"Our boy can't speak words—
  he goes BOING BOING instead!"

"I see," said the doctor,
"it's just as you said.
He doesn't speak words—
he goes BOING BOING instead!

"I've no cure for this.
I can't handle the case."
And he packed up his pills
and walked out of the place.

Then months passed, and Gerald
got louder and louder
Till one day he went *BOOM!*
like a big keg of powder!

It was then that his father
   said, "This is enough!
He'll drive us both mad
   with this terrible stuff!
A boy of his age
   shouldn't sound like a fool.
He's got to learn words.
   We must send him to school."

So Gerald marched off,
an obedient creature,

But he soon was back home
with a note from the teacher.
"From Public School Seven
to Mrs. McCloy:

Your little son Gerald's
a most hopeless boy.
We cannot accept him,
for we have a rule
That pupils must not go
**Cuckoo** in our school.
Your boy will go **HONK**
all his life, I'm afraid.
Sincerely yours, Fanny Schultz,
Teacher, First Grade."

And as little Gerald
grew older, he found
When a fellow goes **BAM!**
no one wants him around.

When a fellow goes SKREEK!
he won't have any friends.
For once he says, "CLANG CLANG CLANG!"
all the fun ends.

CLANG
CLANG

"Nyah nyah!" they all shouted,
"Your name's not McCloy!
You're Gerald McBoing Boing,
the noise-making boy!"

Poor Gerald decided
that he had no place
At home, in the school—
in the whole human race!

And so he concluded
that, drear and forlorn,
He would just disappear
in the thick of a storm.

But as he was boarding
a slow-moving freight,
A voice from the darkness
called out, "Stop, boy! Wait!"

"Aren't you Gerald McBoing Boing,
   the lad who makes squeaks?
My boy, 1 have searched
   for you many long weeks!
1 can make you the most
   famous lad in the nation,
For 1 own the **BONG-BONG-BONG**
   Radio Station!

"I need a smart fellow
to make all the sounds,
Who can **bark** like a dog,
and **bay** like the hounds!

"Your GONG is terrific,
  your toot is inspired!
Quick come to BONG-BONG-BONG,
  McBoing Boing—you're hired!"

Now his parents, proud parents,
　　are able to boast
That their Gerald's *CLOP-CLOP, BANG!*
　　is known coast to coast.

Now Gerald is rich,
   he has friends, he's well fed,
'Cause he doesn't speak words,
   he goes BOING BOING instead!